**W9-BWU-736**

JF Elliott
Elliott, Rebecca.
Bo's magical new friend

5|20

2019

on1081336579          02/21/2020

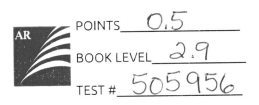

POINTS ___O.5___

BOOK LEVEL ___2.9___

TEST # ___505956___

# Bo's Magical New Friend

# Read more
# UNICORN DIARIES
# books!

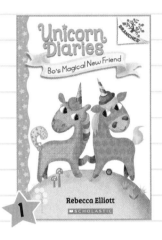

Unicorn Diaries

Bo's Magical New Friend

Rebecca Elliott

SCHOLASTIC

**1**

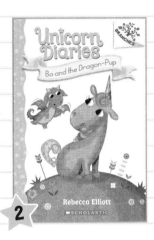

Unicorn Diaries

Bo and the Dragon-Pup

Rebecca Elliott

SCHOLASTIC

**2**

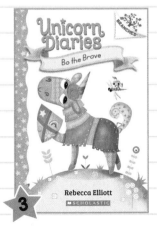

Unicorn Diaries

Bo the Brave

Rebecca Elliott

SCHOLASTIC

**3**

Unicorn Diaries

The Goblin Princess

Rebecca Elliott

SCHOLASTIC

**4**

# Unicorn Diaries

## Bo's Magical New Friend

### Rebecca Elliott

BRANCHES

SCHOLASTIC INC.

For my three magical creatures: Toby, Benjy,
and Clemmie. Xxx — R.E.

Special thanks to Kyle Reed
for his contributions to this book.

All rights reserved. Published by Scholastic Inc., *Publishers since 1920.*
SCHOLASTIC, BRANCHES, and associated logos are trademarks
and/or registered trademarks of Scholastic Inc.

The publisher does not have any control over and does not assume
any responsibility for author or third-party websites or their content.

Library of Congress Cataloging-in-Publication Data Available

Names: Elliott, Rebecca, author.
Title: Bo's magical new friend / by Rebecca Elliott.
Description: First edition. | New York, NY : Branches/Scholastic Inc., 2020.
| Series: Unicorn diaries ; 1 | Summary: Rainbow Tinseltail (called Bo) and the other
students at Sparklegrove School for Unicorns are excited when a brand new
unicorn, Sunny Huckleberry, enters the school, but Sunny does not know
what his special magical power is, and the thought that he might not have
any power at all is making him unhappy; Bo (whose power is granting
wishes) is eager to help him — even though he does not seem to want Bo's help.

Identifiers: LCCN 2018060394| ISBN 9781338323320 (pbk. : alk. paper) | ISBN
9781338323337 (hardcover : alk. paper)
Subjects: LCSH: Unicorns—Juvenile fiction. | Magic—Juvenile fiction. |
Helping behavior—Juvenile fiction. | Diaries—Juvenile fiction. | CYAC:
Unicorns—Fiction. | Magic—Fiction. | Helpfulness—Fiction. |
Diaries—Fiction.
Classification: LCC PZ7.E45812 Bo 2020 | DDC [Fic]—dc23 LC record available at
https://lccn.loc.gov/2018060394

10 9 8 7 6 5 4 3 2 1          20 21 22 23 24

Printed in China   62
First edition, January 2020

Edited by Katie Carella
Book design by Maria Mercado

# Table of Contents

# Nice to Meet You!

Sunday

Hello, new diary!
We're going to be the BEST of friends! But first, you need to know all about me. So here we go!

My name is Rainbow Tinseltail. Everyone calls me Bo.

# I live in Sparklegrove Forest.

Rainbow Falls

Troll Caves

Glimmer Glade

Sparklegrove School for Unicorns

Dragon Nests

Budbloom Meadow

Snowbelle Mountain

Unipods

Fairy Village

Twinkleplop
Lagoon

Goblin
Castle

Lots of magical creatures live here . . .

Like trolls! Here are four things I know about trolls:

They live in caves.

They set up nets. (To catch anyone going near their caves!)

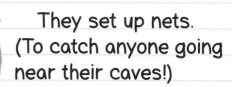

They do not like getting wet.

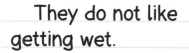

They love moldy cheese. (Yuck!)

Now back to me! I am a unicorn.

**Horn**
Makes a great night-light!
Good for pointing at things!

**Rainbow Mane**
Keeps our necks warm!
(And looks pretty!)

**Nose**
Can sneeze
glitter!

**Tail**
Swishing it makes our Unicorn Power work.
Perfect for swatting away flies!

Unicorns are SO MUCH more than a sparkly horn! Here are some fun facts:

We each have a different Unicorn Power. I'm a Wish Unicorn.

I can grant one wish every week!

We glow when we're nervous.

We sleep on small floating clouds.
(Our snoring sounds like music!)

We eat brightly colored food.

I live at Sparklegrove School for Unicorns. S.S.U. is the best school in the world!

This is Mr. Rumptwinkle. He looks after us and teaches us how to be better unicorns.

I have lots of friends! Here we are outside our **UNIPOD** (where we sleep):

My friends are my family. This is because unicorns don't have moms or dads. We're not born like other creatures are. We just **POP** into the world on really starry nights!

We study **TWINKLE-TASTIC** subjects like:

MAGICAL MOVEMENT
AND MUSIC

MANE AND TAIL
STYLING

CREATURES OF SPARKLEGROVE FOREST

USE OF UNICORN POWERS

Remember how I said we appear on really starry nights? There's a <u>super twinkly</u> sky tonight. I hope there'll be a new unicorn tomorrow!

Diary, can I tell you something? I've never really had a <u>best</u> friend. How great would it be if a new unicorn turned out to be my bestie?!

My **HOOVES** are crossed!

## 2

### A New Friend?

Monday

I have **GLITTERY-GOOD** news, Diary! Guess what popped into the forest last night? A brand-new unicorn!

He trotted into our classroom — and knocked over Mr. Rumptwinkle's desk!

OOPS!

The new unicorn laughed, so we did, too. I guess he's a bit clumsy!

Students, I'd like you to meet Sunny Huckleberry. I'm sure you remember how scary everything was when you were new. So please be kind to Sunny and help him find his way around.

Um, hi!

Hi, Sunny!

We all told him our names.

Sunny sat next to me. Yay!

Then Mr. Rumptwinkle gave Sunny a patch blanket.

I explained how each week we try to earn a new patch for our blankets. When our blankets are full, we're ready to leave school.

Mr. Rumptwinkle always announces what the new patch will be on Mondays. And he gives out the patches on Fridays, at the Patch Parade.

This will be an easy patch for me to get! All I have to do is grant a wish to someone who needs it.

We were excited to use our Unicorn Powers this week. So we told Sunny about our different powers.

I'm a Healer Unicorn. I can make you feel better.

I'm a Thingamabob Unicorn. If you need something, I can find it in my mane.

I'm a Flying Unicorn!

I'm a Weather Unicorn. If you want it to snow, just ask me!

I'm a Size-Changer Unicorn!

Finally, it was my turn.

I'm a Wish Unicorn. I can grant one wish every week. So if there is anything you would like to wish for — anything at all — let me know!

To our surprise, a mouse spoke up next.

I'm a Shape-Shifter Unicorn!

It was Mr. Rumptwinkle of course!
He always makes us jump when he does
that!

It's okay, Sunny. Most — but not all — unicorns know their power as soon as they appear. It might just take you a little longer to find yours.

Then Sunny sneezed and knocked over three desks.

Oops. Well, I know my Unicorn Power is <u>not</u> keeping things neat and tidy!

At **CLOUDTIME**, I whispered an idea to Piper.

I hope Sunny asks me for a wish to know his power. That would help him <u>and</u> I would get my patch.

Yes, but you can't <u>tell</u> people what to wish for. Remember? That's not how your power works.

I know. I just really hope Sunny makes a wish.

Sunny sleeps on the cloud next to mine. He's so funny — he is already snoring!

# Naughty Trolls!

**Tuesday**

Hi Diary,

Today we trotted around Sparklegrove Forest, exploring the woods and looking for creatures to help.

First, we went swimming in Twinkleplop Lagoon.

When Sunny jumped in, he made a HUGE splash!

Then we went sledding down Snowbelle Mountain.

Next, we played on the stepping stones at Rainbow Falls.

Finally, we ended up over near the troll caves.

We quietly **TIP-HOOVED** past their caves.

We stopped in Glimmer Glade for a picnic lunch and ate **SUNBEAM** ice cream. Yum!

Then we had **GLITTERRIFIC** fun playing hide-and-seek.

Here I come!

But – DISASTER! We couldn't find Sunny or Monty anywhere! We looked for AGES and started to feel nervous.

Just then, a tiny Monty ran over. He looked worried!

We asked Monty what happened.

Sunny and I ran over there to hide, but we got swept up in a net!

Trolls!

Yes! I used my Unicorn Power to shrink myself so I could get help. Come quick!

As we galloped after Monty, magic popping sparkles sprang up around him.

We followed Monty to the troll caves.

Eek! We're too late!

The trolls spotted Sunny!

Quick! We need a rescue plan!

What do we know about trolls?

GRUNT! GRUNT!

We thought back to Mr. Rumptwinkle's
CREATURES OF SPARKLEGROVE FOREST lessons.

Trolls hate water!

Yes! I'll use my Unicorn Power to make it rain!

Hurry!

Jed swished his tail. Suddenly, storm clouds filled the sky and rain poured down.

Everyone laughed.

Scarlett swished her tail. Then she pulled something from her mane.

Ta-da! Scissors are the perfect thingamabob for this job!

But the net is high up. How will we reach it?

I can help!

Sunny fell to the ground as popping sparkles swirled around Scarlett and Nutmeg.

*TWINKLE-POP!*

Yay! Piper earned her new patch!

When we got back to school, we all ate **CLOUD FLUFF** pie.

Sunny, I'm so glad you're okay. And you kept smiling! How are you so super brave?

If you smile, things sometimes don't seem so bad. Even being trapped in a big scary troll net!

It is great that everyone has earned their patches now! Well, everyone except for me and Sunny. At **CLOUDTIME**, I tried to hint to Sunny that I could help him find out his power . . .

If only I knew what my power was.

If only <u>someone</u> would make a WISH to learn their power . . . Sunny?

But he was already snoring. I'll try again tomorrow!

# 4
## The Fairy Party

Hello Diary,
    At breakfast, I talked to Nutmeg about Sunny.

Why doesn't Sunny just wish to know his power? It would be so easy for me to help him.

That's a big favor to ask. Maybe he doesn't feel like he knows you well enough?

I trotted over to Sunny after class.

We stopped to smell the flowers in Budbloom Meadow.

We galloped past Goblin Castle.

The goblin royal family lives there.

Oooo. I hear it's hard to find food at the castle.

Really? Why?

Because the goblins keep GOBLIN' everything up!!

HAHAHAHA HAHA!

HEHEHEHE HEHE!

Finally, we reached Fairy Village.

It's so teeny and cute!

A Fairy Warrior flew out from behind a leaf. He looked mad!

Who are you calling <u>cute</u>?

No one, sir!

GRR!

<u>You</u> don't look cute at all!!

Who would turn down a fairy party??

We danced the night away. It was MAGICAL!

The fairies' band –The Flutter-byes – sounded <u>so</u> good that we invited them to play at our Patch Parade on Friday!

THE FLUTTER -BYES

Then we looked up at the twinkly stars together.

I wanted to help Sunny – not only because I wanted my new patch, but also because he's my friend. I decided NOW was the time to talk to him about making a wish . . .

I've had the best time with you today, Sunny.

I know! Me too!

I was kind of hoping that if we spent more time together, you might ask _me_ to help you find out what your power is.

Wait a minute. Is that the only reason you hung out with me today? So I would ask you for a wish? You just wanted to earn your patch?

But he trotted away, back to our **UNIPOD**.

Oh, Diary, I have made a mess of things! Sunny thinks I only wanted to be his friend because of some silly patch. The truth is, more than anything, I want to be a good friend to Sunny. How can I fix this?

## 5

### Funny Sunny

Thursday

Mr. Rumptwinkle brought teeny-
weeny tree sprites to our CREATURES OF
SPARKLEGROVE FOREST class today. We were
all excited to see them up close. But
Piper was scared of them.

Sunny pretended he didn't know a tree sprite was sitting on his head.

What? Do I have something stuck in my teeth? How embarrassing.

Piper laughed so hard, she wasn't scared anymore!

HA! HA! HA! HA! HA!

We had MAGICAL MOVEMENT AND MUSIC class next. We were all dancing, but Monty hid in the corner.

Sunny fell over a lot — until Monty joined in. They started laughing! Then they did a funny dance together.

In MANE AND TAIL STYLING class, Mr. Rumptwinkle taught us a cool new braid. Nutmeg got in a tangle!

Argh! I'm stuck!

Sunny kept Nutmeg calm while Mr. Rumptwinkle untied her.

Sunny was a great friend to everyone today. But I think he's still a bit upset with me.

I have an idea, Diary! I'm going to make something special for Sunny – to show what a good friend I can be.

I grabbed my yarn and worked hard all evening!

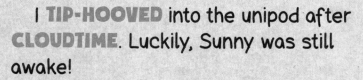

I **TIP-HOOVED** into the unipod after **CLOUDTIME**. Luckily, Sunny was still awake!

Sunny, I made a special patch just for you. You deserve one for making everyone laugh when they really needed to today.

Wow, Bo! Thank you. That's really sparkly sweet of you!

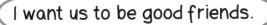

I want us to be good friends.

I know. I'm sorry I ran off yesterday.

It's just that you all have such cool powers. What if mine is terrible? Plus, I want to find out my power on my own like all of you — not with a wish. Is that okay?

Of course. I totally understand.

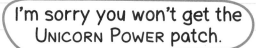

I'm sorry you won't get the UNICORN POWER patch.

And I'm sorry I'm not helping you earn your patch by asking for a wish.

Hey, that's okay. I got a new friend this week. There's no patch better than that.

Nothing is better than that!

We stayed up late talking and laughing. It was <u>so</u> cool to hang out with my new friend!

Sunny is always trying to make others happy. I want him to be happy, too! I hope he finds his power in time for tomorrow's Patch Parade . . . Good night, Diary!

# 6

## The Unicorn Power Patch

**Friday**

Everyone is excited about tonight's Patch Parade! Well, except for Mr. Rumptwinkle . . . He lost his favorite necktie somewhere near the troll caves!

At lunch, everyone was talking about the parade.

I can't wait to get my new patch!

Look how many I have already!

Oh, sorry, Bo and Sunny.

We forgot you're not getting patches tonight.

We all trotted to Budbloom Meadow.

The Patch Parade was SUPER! The Flutter-byes played. And we ate my favorite foods — **DREAM DUST, MAGIC MALLOWS,** and **TWIRL DROPS!**

At one point, Sunny tripped and a
huge bowl of TWINKLEBERRY ice cream
flew into the air!

SPLAT!

We were laughing our **TAILS** off!

You may not know your Unicorn Power yet, Sunny. But the power of laughter is better than <u>any</u> magical power! You totally deserve that special patch I made for you.

My tail started twirling round. **SWISH!**
A new shiny drum appeared. Then –

I finally earned my patch! I felt so
happy! We all danced and drank sugar
berry syrup. Sunny had never had syrup
before – it made him hiccup loudly!

Diary, you won't believe what happened!

Sunny hiccupped once more, and – **PING!** We could see him again!

I've got an idea! Mr. Rumptwinkle, I'm going to find your necktie.

But it's near the troll caves! It is too dangerous there!

Trolls can't catch me if they can't see me!

**HICCUP!** Then we all heard Sunny galloping away...

He came back a few minutes later
with Mr. Rumptwinkle's necktie!

Wow! Thank you, Sunny!
That was really clever and brave.

TWINKLE-POP!

Sunny earned his first patch all on his
own – and just in time!
**HOORAY!**

At the end of the night, we paraded past Mr. Rumptwinkle to finally collect our new patches.

Then we danced under the twinkling sky until our **HOOVES** hurt.

Phew! This was a BIG week! I got a new patch, my school got a new unicorn (who has the COOLEST power EVER!), and most important of all . . . I GOT A <u>BEST</u> FRIEND!

See you next time, Diary! Have super sweet and sparkly dreams!

**Rebecca Elliott** may not have a magical horn or sneeze glitter, but she's still a lot like a unicorn. Rebecca always tries to have a positive attitude, she likes to laugh a lot, and she lives with some great creatures — her guitar-playing husband, noisy-yet-charming children, crazy chickens, and a big, lazy cat called Bernard. She gets to hang out with these fun characters and write stories for a living, so she thinks her life is pretty magical!

Rebecca is the author of JUST BECAUSE, MR. SUPER POOPY PANTS, and the *USA Today* bestselling early chapter book series OWL DIARIES.

# Unicorn Diaries

## How much do you know about Bo's Magical New Friend?

Reread Chapter 1. What are five fun facts about unicorns?

The unicorns of S.S.U. earn new patches every week. What happens when a unicorn has earned their patch? What does it mean when their patch blanket is full?

Bo tries to make Sunny feel welcome at school by explaining the rules and showing him around the forest. What are two ways that you could help make a new friend feel welcome?

Sunny feels sad when he thinks Bo only wants to be his friend to earn a patch. How does Bo make Sunny feel better?

If you were a magical unicorn, what power would you have? Draw, label, and name your unicorn!